THE RAND McNALLY BOOK OF
Favorite Pillowtime Tales

RAND McNALLY & COMPANY · Chicago

Established 1856

CONTENTS

MR. BEAR'S HOUSE

ONCE UPON A TIME there was a bear who lived
in a cave in the woods. He was a fat brown
bear and he liked to go walking. One day he
walked to the edge of town. He heard a great
hammering noise and, peeking out between the
leaves of the bushes, he saw a carpenter building

a house. Mr. Bear was fascinated. Every day he came back to watch. He saw the carpenter hammer the nails. He saw the house grow — walls, roof, windows, and a porch.

"How much prettier than my cave!" Mr. Bear said to himself. "I want a house to live in."

And so Mr. Bear went about the forest collecting pieces of wood until he had a big stack. "Now," he thought, "I need a hammer." And so he made a hammer out of a rock and a stick. "Now," he said, "I need some nails."

And so he walked to the edge of town and looked around the new house. It was late in the day, and the carpenter had gone home. Sure enough, there were some nails lying about on the ground. Mr. Bear picked them up and carried them back to the woods.

Now Mr. Bear was really busy. He hammered and hammered and hammered — one nail after another. The animals in the forest heard the banging noise and came to see what was happening.

"Whatever are you doing?" chirped the robins.

"I'm building a house," said Mr. Bear.

"With wood and such noise!" The birds shook their heads. "We use grasses and we don't make any noise at all."

"But I'm too big for a nest," said Mr. Bear.

The beavers from the pond came over next. "Whatever are you doing?" they asked.

"I'm building a house," explained Mr. Bear.

"We use mud, not nails, to hold our house together," said the beavers.

"Mud wouldn't be strong enough for my house," Mr. Bear told them.

"But," noticed one old beaver, "the wind will blow through the cracks in your house."

Mr. Bear stopped work and surveyed his walls. Yes, there *were* cracks between the logs, and he

could see daylight shining through. He shook his head sadly.

"It won't be as warm as a cave," ventured a timid deer.

Mr. Bear looked quite disappointed.

"Let's all help Mr. Bear," the old beaver suggested. "We beavers will put mud in the cracks."

"Oh, thank you!" Mr. Bear smiled happily, and the beavers hurried to the pond to fetch some mud. They put the mud in the cracks and smoothed it with their broad tails until no more daylight came shining through.

Finally the four walls of the house were built, with spaces for windows and a door.

"The rain can come in," said the rabbits who had come to watch. "We don't have rain in our houses."

"I need a roof," Mr. Bear explained to them. But he himself was puzzled. How could he ever put a roof over his four walls?

"We'll help you," sang the birds. "We'll make your roof."

"How?" asked Mr. Bear.

"We'll weave a roof with long grasses — a thatched roof."

Mr. Bear smiled his thanks.

It took a long time for the birds to make the big thatched roof that Mr. Bear needed. While they gathered the grass and wove it together, Mr.

Bear was busy putting in his floor. *Hammer, hammer, hammer! Bang, bang, bang!* The noise echoed through the woods.

As Mr. Bear put the last nail into his floor, a bluejay flew over his head. "The roof is finished and ready to put on," he called.

In a minute hundreds of birds came flying and fluttering through the woods. They carried the new roof in their beaks. The bluejay waited until it was exactly over the top of the four walls. "Now," he shouted, "drop it!" The birds opened their beaks and the roof fell into place.

"How splendid! How splendid!" Mr. Bear danced in glee. Then he went ahead and made his door.

His house really looked like a house now. But there were still no windows — just big openings where the windows should fit.

"The rain can come in the windows," said the beavers, shaking their heads.

"The house will be cold," sighed the rabbits.

Mr. Bear was dismayed. "I shall have to ask the carpenter about windows," he decided. And so he walked to the edge of town again.

There he saw the carpenter building another house.

"Mr. Carpenter," he called.

The carpenter looked surprised. He put down his hammer, climbed down his ladder, and asked, "Did you call me?"

Mr. Bear nodded. "Yes, please, I did."

"I never met a talking bear before—" began the carpenter, scratching his head.

"All I want to know," said Mr. Bear, "is how to put a window in a house."

The carpenter looked bewildered. Then, seeing how serious the bear was, he explained.

"First, we make a frame. Then we putty in the glass."

Mr. Bear frowned. He did not understand.

"Why," the carpenter asked, "do you want to know?"

"Because my house needs windows," answered Mr. Bear.

"Your house?" More amazement showed in the carpenter's face. "Your house?"

"Yes," explained Mr. Bear. "I am building a house, but I can't seem to manage the windows."

"Well," said the carpenter, "if a bear can build

a house, I guess I can put in the windows — and
without charge."

"Oh," exclaimed Mr. Bear, "do you mean that?"

"I certainly do," replied the carpenter.

"Well, then, come and see my house," Mr. Bear
urged.

The carpenter went with him into the forest. There he saw a little house with a thatched roof and a wooden door. He opened the door and stepped inside onto the wooden floor.

"Unbelievable!" he exclaimed. "Why, if I hadn't seen it myself, I would never have believed it."

He went over and looked at the two spaces Mr. Bear had left for his windows.

"Tomorrow morning," announced the carpenter, "I shall be here early to put in your windows."

He shook Mr. Bear's paw and left. Mr. Bear was quite pleased with his kindness. The very next

morning the carpenter came and put in the windows—frame and putty and glass and all. Mr. Bear thanked him warmly as he left.

"Now, Mr. Bear's house is finished," the birds sang.

"No," Mr. Bear told them, "not yet. I have to

make some furniture." And he made a bed, a table, and four chairs.

"Now," said Mr. Bear, "I shall have a party for all my kind friends."

The birds brought berries, the squirrels nuts, the beavers sent some apples, and the rabbits came with carrots. Mr. Bear furnished the honey. He invited the kind carpenter, too, and that good man brought ice cream enough for all.

"Ah, happy day!" sighed Mr. Bear.

And that is how fat brown Mr. Bear came to live in his comfortable little house in the woods.

TUBBY TURTLE

HURRY UP Tubby, or you will be late for school again," said Mrs. Turtle. Tubby was trying to get his necktie on straight. Finally he gave up and started out with one end dragging on the ground.

He hadn't gone far when Rabbit jumped
ahead of him. "Wait for me, Rabbit," Tubby
called. "Sorry," said Rabbit, "but I've got to
keep hop-hop-hopping or I won't get to
school on time."

"Hi, Squirrel, wait for me," Tubby called as Squirrel leaped past. "Sorry," said Squirrel, "but if I wait for you, we will both be late."

The teacher was ringing the school bell
when Rabbit and Squirrel arrived. "Have
you seen Tubby?" asked Miss Owl.

"He's coming as fast as a snail," they told
her. "He must be halfway here by now."

Rabbit and Squirrel didn't know that just as Tubby reached the top of the hill he stepped on a loose stone. The stone rolled him downhill twice as fast as he had come up. No wonder that Tubby was later than usual for school.

The singing lesson was almost over when he came in. Rabbit and Squirrel sang the low notes while Possum and Chipmunk took the high notes.

Tubby didn't know the words or the music so he started singing "la-la-la," hoping no one would notice him. He couldn't understand why the class suddenly burst out laughing.

Miss Owl rapped sharply on her desk. "Come to order," she said, as she gave Tubby a black mark for being so late. "Now class, it is time for you to recite your pieces. Who wants to be first?"

Rabbit hopped up quickly, took a bow and recited,

"Roses are red, violets are blue,
But I like carrots in my stew."

Squirrel came next. With a saucy flick of his tail, he spoke,

"Some like it hot, some like it cold,
But I like acorns five days old."

Tubby listened while Possum and Chipmunk recited their verses. Then it was
Tubby's turn. It took him a long time to
remember the words. He spoke slowly,

"I'm just a clumsy turtle
Beneath a heavy shell,
But I wish-wish-wish with all my heart
I *could* do something well."

"Everyone can do something worthwhile if they think about it enough," said Miss Owl. "You musn't get discouraged, Tubby." Just then the clock struck ten. That meant recess and time for cookies.

"Let me get the cookies," said Rabbit,

jumping to reach the top shelf. He put the bag on Miss Owl's desk without spilling a single crumb.

"It's my turn to open the bag," said Squirrel. His sharp teeth quickly ripped the paper apart.

"Here are the plates," said Possum and Chipmunk. They gave a shiny grape leaf to each one. Tubby was anxious to help too, but there wasn't a thing he could do.

"I'm no good to anyone," he thought as he quietly nibbled the edge of his cookie.

Rabbit and Squirrel had cleaned up their plates in a hurry. They were already out in the schoolyard, chasing each other in circles.

Tubby, as usual, trailed far behind as the others went hoppity-skippity down the hill to the water lily pond. "Watch this!" Squirrel called back to Tubby.

Squirrel took a flying leap. He planned to catch hold of a willow branch above the water. The plan didn't work. He missed the branch and flew headfirst into the pond. His feet got tangled in the water lily stems.

Rabbit tried to fish him out with a long pole. When Squirrel grabbed the pole, Rabbit lost his balance. There was a big splash as Rabbit disappeared in the water.

Tubby got there just in time. Without waiting to take off his necktie he swam out

to his friends. "Stop sputtering and thrashing," he called.

"Put your paws on my back, Rabbit. Now Squirrel, grab hold of my tail and kick your hind legs free." In two minutes Tubby helped them safely to shore.

"We had a narrow escape," Rabbit panted.
"Where would you be now if Tubby had
not come to the rescue?" asked Possum and
Chipmunk.

Squirrel's teeth chattered with cold as he
and Rabbit thanked Tubby again and again.

Tubby's eyes were blinking with happiness. He had thought of a new verse to recite,

"I'm just a clumsy turtle
Beneath a heavy shell,
But I'm glad-glad-glad with all my heart
I *can* do something well."

CHESTER, THE LITTLE PONY

CHESTER was a pony on Farmer Miller's farm. He was a young pony with a warm, brown coat, a shaggy mane, and a long, thick tail which he swished around to chase the flies away on a summer day. Farmer Miller gave Chester a good home. He saw that he had plenty of fresh, cool water to drink and hay and oats to eat. But Chester was not quite happy. He had no one to play with. Farmer Miller had cows and a goat and chickens and ducks and a dog named Scott. But he did not have a horse—he had a tractor and tractors are not much fun for ponies. So Chester was a lonesome pony.

Farmer Miller liked the pony but, when Chester was full-grown, he could not keep him any more. If Chester had been a horse, he might have pulled the plow and the thresher and earned his keep on the farm.

But he was just a pony and he could not do hard work. So Farmer Miller went to see a man who owned other ponies. His name was Baxter, and he bought Chester from Farmer Miller and put him in the stable along with his other ponies. On Saturdays and Sundays and holidays little boys and girls were taken for rides on Mr. Baxter's ponies, around and around in a circle.

The first time Mr. Baxter put a saddle on Chester's back, Chester was very frightened. He jumped and kicked and tried to shake it off. After a while he got used to it. Later Mr. Baxter put his boy Tim in the saddle and led Chester around and around.

Chester liked it and soon, when he walked around the circle with the other ponies on Saturdays and Sundays and holidays carrying little boys and girls on his back, he felt very happy. He grew to love the children and wanted to be with them all the time.

But on all the days except Saturdays
and Sundays and holidays Chester stayed
in the stable most of the time. There were
other ponies to keep him company and he
was given good care with fresh water and
hay and oats. Still, he did not like to stay

indoors so much. He wondered where all the little boys and girls might be who came to ride him on Saturdays and Sundays and holidays and why they did not come on other days. He could not know that "Baxter's Rides" was open only on Saturdays and Sundays and holidays.

BAXTER'S RIDES
OPEN ONLY ON SATURDAYS, SUNDAYS AND HOLIDAYS

One afternoon Chester had been taken out for a short run and then led back to his stall in the stable. He was thinking of all the children who would have liked a pony ride and he was wondering where all the little boys and girls might be. After a while he noticed that Mr. Baxter had forgotten to

tie him in his stall. So he went to the stable door. When he gave it a push, the door opened and—out went Chester. He was surprised to be outside but also pleased. He thought that maybe he could go and find some of the boys and girls who would like to have a pony ride.

Mr. Baxter was in the house and did not see Chester wander away. Chester knew that the children did not live in Mr. Baxter's house—only Tim lived there with his father. Soon it got dark and Chester could not see very well. But he saw lights from some houses in the distance. He thought he had better go there and look for the children.

A little light came from the back of the first house, and Chester thought he would go up the back steps. But, when he tried to

go up the stairs, he could not do it. Ponies cannot climb stairs! There were several large empty milk bottles on the stairs. Chester was so clumsy that he stumbled and knocked over one bottle, which in turn knocked over all the other bottles. The bottles made a terrible noise as they bumped down the steps. They rolled on down the hill, banging against rocks and rattling and clattering.

The noise scared Chester so that he ran away as fast as he could go. The people in the house heard the big commotion and rushed out to see what had happened. They saw the empty bottles rumbling and clanging and crashing away until they hit some trees with a loud BOOM-BOOM! But by that time Chester was disappearing fast down the road and they did not even hear his hoofs as he galloped away.

Chester was dismayed but not discouraged. When he came to the next house, he was careful not to go near the stairs. He walked searchingly around the house. Now, the mother who lived there had washed the family clothes that day and left the wash

on the line to dry until she had finished the
evening chores. In the dark Chester walked
right into the clothesline. When it stopped
him, he was quite annoyed and pushed with
all his might. SNAP! The line broke, and
all the fine clean clothes fell on the ground

except a big white sheet which landed right over Chester's head and back. This frightened Chester greatly and into a gallop he went, fast away. The people in the house heard the noise and ran out, but all they could see were the nice, clean clothes scat-

tered on the ground and a white sheet flying away down the road. The people were scared, too, for they could not see that it was only Chester running so fast. After a few blocks the big sheet sailed off Chester's back and landed like a parachute among some bushes.

Chester now realized that, if he were to find the boys and girls to take for a pony ride, he would have to be more careful. So, when he came to the third house, he just walked quietly up to a window where a light was shining. Sure enough, there were children inside—a whole lot of them, playing with blocks and dolls and trains. They looked so kind and friendly he wondered how he could make them come out for a ride.

"NEIGH-NEIGH," he said, "NEIGH-NEIGH," and he pressed his nose close to the window-pane. Suddenly one of the little boys looked up and cried, "A horse!" And then the

mother looked at the window and let out a scream, for there was Chester's nose flat against the glass and his ears sticking up above his big, curious eyes. The father quickly telephoned to the village police and said: "Help! A wild horse is breaking through our window!" And then the police came in the police car with shrieking sirens and heavy clubs. But Chester could not take his eyes away from the nice children and,

when the police came, there was the pony still staring at the little boys and girls through the window and wondering how he could make them come out for a pony ride.

The police said: "Why, it's only a little pony!" And when the children saw Chester, they said: "It's the pony from 'Baxter's Rides'! It's the pony we ride on Saturdays and Sundays and holidays! Please, may we take him back to Mr. Baxter?" So they put a rope around Chester's neck and they all led him back to the stable.

Mr. Baxter had missed Chester and was afraid he had lost his best pony, whom the children liked to ride better than any of the other ponies. He was glad when they brought Chester home, and he patted him and gave him extra oats for his supper.

Then he said to the children: "Perhaps

Chester went away because he was lonesome for boys and girls. Maybe he wants you children to ride him every day and not only on Saturdays and Sundays and holidays. Could you come and ride him on the other days, too?"

The father and mother said yes, and the children said why, of course, they would love to ride him every single day in the week. And so, every day thereafter, they went to Mr. Baxter's stable and took Chester out for nice, long pony rides. And from that time on Chester was a happy pony.

CHOO-CHOO,
THE LITTLE SWITCH ENGINE

CHOO-CHOO, the Little Switch Engine, was very happy. He worked in the railroad yard of a large city, where there were many, many tracks running along side by side. Here and there a track crossed over and ran into another track. These places were called switches, and the men who made a train on one track cross over onto another track were called switchmen.

Choo-choo's work was to push freight cars over the switches onto different tracks. There were many cars on the long freight trains that came into the big city, and this was the way they were sorted out. The cars which were to go one way were pushed onto one track. The cars which were to go another way were pushed onto another track. Then a big, strong, puffing freight engine would fasten

himself to each line of cars, and off they all would go to some faraway city.

Choo-choo always felt very proud of himself when he saw a big freight engine pulling a long train away.

"If it weren't for me, he wouldn't find cars all ready for him to take out," the happy Little Switch Engine said to himself.

After he had worked for many, many days in the big railroad yard, Choo-choo began to dream of the time when he would grow up.

At first he hoped to grow up into a big, strong, puffing freight engine. He would pull long trains of freight cars from one big city to another.

Then Choo-choo began to think it might be more fun to grow up into a big, shining, streamlined passenger engine. He would carry cars with people in them instead of freight.

Over at the edge of the railroad yard there were some long, straight tracks. They were the "main lines" which stretched for miles and miles to other big cities. Only the trains that were going to faraway cities could use these tracks.

Every day great, shining, streamlined passenger trains rushed by on these main lines. They went so fast that Choo-choo did not even have a chance to say, "How do you do?" Sometimes he would call *toot-toot!* to them with his little whistle. And sometimes they would answer back with a single *toot!*

from their big whistles. But it was a long time before Choo-choo had a chance to talk with one of them.

It all happened one day when Choo-choo was at the roundhouse. This was a place where engine doctors took care of engines which had something the matter with them. Choo-choo had a little leak in his boiler, and he was going to have it fixed.

A fine, big, streamlined passenger engine stood beside him on the track in the roundhouse. This engine was waiting to have something fixed, too. At first Choo-choo felt a little bashful. But the big engine was very friendly. Soon he was telling the Little Switch Engine all about the faraway cities he had been to. "Passenger engines are the most important of all," he said proudly.

"That's just what I thought," Choo-choo said. "And that's why I have decided that, when I grow up, I shall be a great, shining, streamlined passenger engine like you, instead of just a big freight engine."

"When you grow up!" cried the big passenger engine, so surprised that he hardly knew what to say. And then, all at once, he began to laugh. He laughed and laughed, as though he had just heard the funniest joke in all the world.

"What is so funny about that?" Choo-choo asked.

"What is so funny—*ho-ho!*" snorted the big engine. "Why, you little simpleton, people and dogs grow up, but an engine always stays just as he is made. Who ever heard of an engine growing up? What a little simpleton you are!"

Little Choo-choo had always been happy, but now he became sad, because he could no longer dream of growing up. The engine doctor at the roundhouse fixed his boiler, and Choo-choo went

back to the railroad yard. But Choo-choo was so sad that he could not work.

He did his work so poorly that another switch engine came to take his place. And poor little Choo-choo was pushed onto a sidetrack near the roundhouse. There he stood, sad and alone, and with nothing at all to do. He did not much care what happened to him, now that he knew he could never grow up into a big passenger engine—or even into a big freight engine.

One day a new engineer and fireman came up to Choo-choo as he stood sadly on the sidetrack. The fireman climbed into the Little Switch Engine and built a fire. The engineer walked all around the Little Switch Engine and squirted oil into him with a big oilcan. As soon as the fire made steam in the boiler, the engineer told the fireman to ring the bell. Then he backed little Choo-choo off the sidetrack.

They filled his tender with coal—as much as he could carry. And they filled his water tank with water—as much as he could drink. The engineer looked again at a piece of paper, to make sure he had his orders right. Then he ran Choo-choo out to a main-line track.

"We can make it all the way without having to sidetrack," he told the fireman, "if this little old teapot doesn't give us any trouble."

Choo-choo wondered what the engineer meant. Then he realized that he, Choo-choo, the Little Switch Engine, was being called a little old teapot!

"The very idea!" he said to himself, and he became quite angry. "I'll just show them that I am as good as any other engine. A little old teapot, indeed!"

Choo-choo forgot all about being sad and he began to work as well as he had ever worked in his whole life. When the engineer opened the throttle wide, Choo-choo began to run as fast as he could run—faster than he had ever run before.

The first thing he knew, Choo-choo was out in the country. His small, heavy wheels turned so

fast that they looked like tops spinning along on their sides. Suddenly Choo-choo found that he was happy again. For here he was, speeding along the main line, just like one of the big streamlined passenger engines.

"I don't know where they are taking me," he laughed to himself, "but this is wonderful!"

As he went along, Choo-choo listened to what the engineer and fireman were saying to each other. Before long he found out where he was going. A town along the railroad needed a switch engine in its little railroad yard. And Choo-choo was being sent to this smaller town, because he no longer seemed able to do the hard work in the big city railroad yard.

Choo-choo was unhappy for a moment when he thought of leaving the big city. Then he smiled again as he saw how fast he could make the fields and woods whiz by. He tooted his whistle for

crossings. He ran past little railroad stations, just as if he were a great, shining, streamlined engine pulling a fine long train of passenger cars.

After several hours he came to the edge of a town. The engineer began to slow Choo-choo down.

"This is our stop, Ben," he said to the fireman.

At the little railroad station the engineer pulled Choo-choo onto a sidetrack and stopped him. Then he walked over to the station to see the stationmaster.

In a moment the engineer came running back, waving a sheet of paper.

"Number 10 is laid up at the next town," he called to the fireman. "Its engine has blown both cylinder heads and is dead on the track. We have orders to sidetrack the dead engine and to let the Little Switch Engine pull the train into the city."

Choo-choo could hardly believe what he heard. Was it really true that he was going to pull a fine long passenger train into the city, just like a big engine?

They turned him around so that he could run backward along the main line to the next town. There Train Number 10 stood waiting, with its big crippled engine.

And to Choo-choo's surprise, who should the crippled engine be but the fine, big, streamlined passenger engine that had laughed at him in the roundhouse!

Choo-choo did not want to make the poor engine feel any worse, but he just could not help saying, "I really must be growing up after all, because they have sent me to pull your train in."

The crippled engine did not laugh at Choo-choo this time.

"Perhaps you are," he said. "You'll show yourself to be a real engine if you can get my train into the city without losing any more time. Your little wheels make you go rather slow, but try to do your best."

Without wasting any time Choo-choo pulled the big crippled engine onto a sidetrack, out of the

way. Next he coupled on the long train of bright
passenger cars. Then he began pulling it toward
the big city.

The train was heavy, but it was not nearly so
hard to pull as some of the freight cars Choo-choo
had pulled in the big railroad yard. The Little

Switch Engine did not mind the work at all. He began to go faster and faster. He would show the big crippled engine!

The fields and woods whizzed by. He tooted his whistle for crossings. He ran past little railroad stations.

At last Choo-choo came to the city. He rushed through the big railroad yard and past the round-house. He whistled merrily—*too-too-o-oot!* Then, under the great train shed of the big passenger station, the engineer stopped the Little Switch Engine.

After the passengers were all out of the cars, Choo-choo was cut loose from the train. He rolled on down through the train shed and was switched onto another track. Then he was run back to the roundhouse.

At the roundhouse the engineer and the fireman told everyone what a fine little switch engine Choo-choo was. They spoke so well of him that he was sent back to the big city railroad yard and given his old work to do. Nothing more was said about his going to the little railroad yard in the smaller town. And no one ever had any fault to find with him or his work again.

Choo-choo was happy once more. It did not matter to him that he was only a Little Switch Engine—that he could never be anything else. He knew that once he had been grown-up enough to pull a fine long train of passenger cars. And he knew he had done it so well that no great, shining, streamlined passenger engine would ever laugh at him again.